ANGELS

COME IN ALL SHAPES AND SIZES

Written and Illustrated by

C.V. SCHWEITZER

Dadielte Productions. 2022

Moreno Valley, Ca

ISBN: 978-0-9981419-4-7

Published and Distributed by

Dadielte Production

P.O. Box 1266

Moreno Valley, CA 92556-1266

Printed and Bound in the United States of America

Written and Illustrated by C.V. Schweitzer

First Printing

This book is dedicated to the animals who found themselves abandoned for no reason other than being the animals they are.

Without careful thought and planning, impulsive purchase for oneself or in too many cases as a gift for another, has bound them to the care of a living creature for years.

What seems like overnight that cute little thing has become much bigger and more demanding.

When their care becomes too much, a responsible person will take them to an animal shelter where they have a chance to find a new loving owner.

Others choose to abandon them on the streets to hunger, thirst, injury and possible death.

This book could not have been published without the help of the following:

Editors:

Anna Christian and Cathy Fortin Jenkins

Junior Editors:

Nicolas Muia and Gabriela Muia

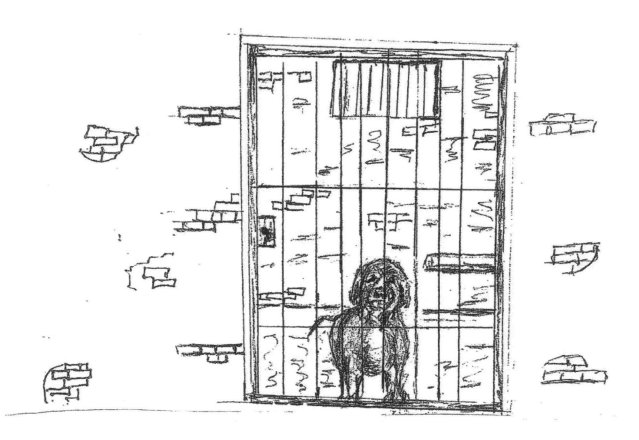

"You be a good dog," Officer Simms said as she shut the holding cell door of the Wilmont County Court House. "I'll be back to get you in a few minutes."

After straining her eyes for several seconds trying to see past the point where Officer Simms disappeared, the young golden retriever circled round several times before she finally lay down on the hard floor.

"So, what are you in for?"

The dog slowly opened one eye. Seeing nothing, she opened the other. Still not seeing where the voice came from, she turned her head from side to side.

"I'm up here on the bench."

When the dog got up and turned around, she found herself face-to-face with a cricket sitting on the corner of a metal bench that was attached to the wall.

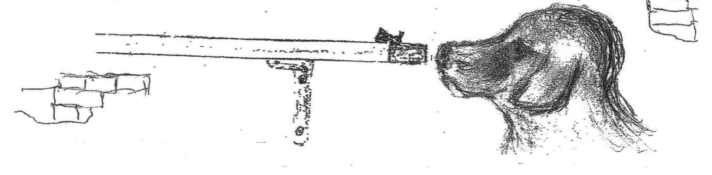

 "Well?" Inquired the cricket.

"You kind of surprised me," the young dog said cocking her head from side to side. "I ah...I've talked to other dogs before and once I thought I heard a bird say something, but I've never talked to a bug."

"Bug, I'm not just any old bug. I'm a cricket."

"I know that," replied the dog. I've seen lots of crickets, but none of them ever talked to me before."

"Well then, let me introduce myself. I'm Finnegan Shamus, the fourth. My friends just call me Fin."

"Why do you talk so funny?"

"Because I'm Irish, that's why. Did you know that crickets bring people good luck?"

"No, I never heard of that."

"Well, it's true. I don't mean to brag, but us Irish crickets are the luckiest of them all."

"Do you think your luck would work for a dog?"

"I don't see why not. Luck is luck in my book. Now that I told you my name, what's yours?"

"Angel, er, Milly. No, Angel."

"Well, which is it?"

"Sandy calls me Angel. It's a long story. That's why we're here." Fin rubbed his feelers together. "Go on."

It all started the week before Christmas. This young couple Bill and Sue Hall bought me from a shopping cart in the parking- lot of the West Wing Mall. They called me Milly after some President's dog.

The first few weeks were great. The smell of the Christmas tree reminded me of the place where I was born. I did however find the flashing light that covered the tree a bit frightening at first.

The Halls played with me all the time back then. Every time I turned around there was a new toy.

Then one day everything changed. The bright colored packages and the beautiful tree were gone along with the Hall's love and affection.

Suddenly, I found myself chained up in the small patio of our apartment. I spent hours and hours trying to figure out why.

One day the loneliness became too much for me, and I began to howl I couldn't help myself. I didn't know what else to do.

The same neighbors who used to pet me and say how cute I was, started shouting and throwing things.

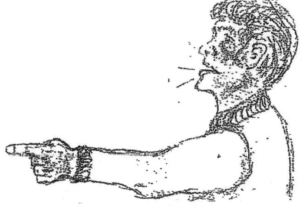

Two weeks ago, the apartment manager came out to the patio with Bill and started shouting and pointing at me and the holes that I had dug. Then he pointed off into space.

The next day Bill came home early. I was so happy when he came out to the patio with my leash. My walk sadly ended in the back seat of the car.

We drove and drove then suddenly stopped. Bill led me into the woods and took off my collar.

When I stopped to check out a new smell, Bill tossed my leash and collar into the bushes, then jumped in the car and sped away.

As I ran after the car, I slipped and fell into the ditch. When I got back up on the road, I was all alone. I saw lights off in the distance and decided to go towards them.

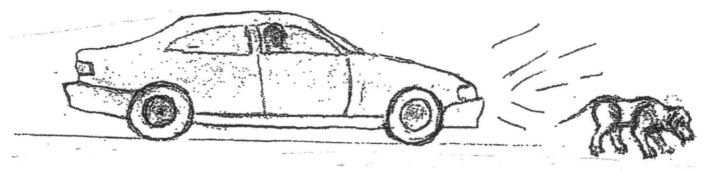

The car ride had made me hungry and thirsty. I ran on and on. It seemed like forever. Then a car roared up from behind me and made me jump.

To escape I ran into an alley behind a large row of buildings.

I finally heard the sound of dripping water coming from a pipe. It tasted awful.

As I continued on down the alley sniffing for food, I was attracted to a trashcan.

The second I put my paws on the rim a cat jumped out. I let out a yelp and ran further down the alley.

I carefully nudged the next trashcan. I finally found a half-eaten pizza.

When I finished, I continued down the alley looking for more food. As I approached the next pile of trash, I heard a sound coming from a box.

It was a sound I had heard many times before when Bill and Sue took me for a walk.

When I put my nose over the side of the box, there it was - a baby human.

It reached out and grabbed the hair on my chest and didn't want to let go.

A strange feeling suddenly came over me.

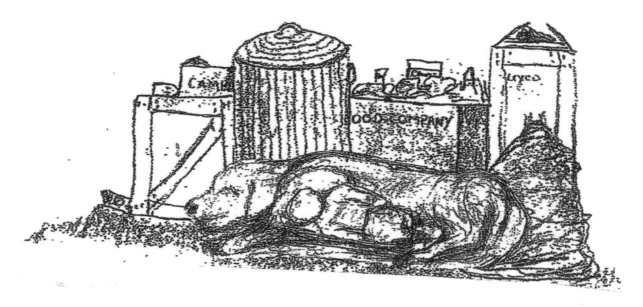

It was as if the baby needed me as much as I needed it!

So, I circled round and round until I had mashed down the sides of the box. Then I lay down beside the baby and went to sleep.

It was just getting light when I heard the unmistakable sound of a trash-truck.

Suddenly, a man was standing over us. I looked up and wagged my tail.

He stared at us for several seconds, then he turned and ran back towards the trash-truck. A few minutes the alley was filled with police cars. The sirens hurt my ears.

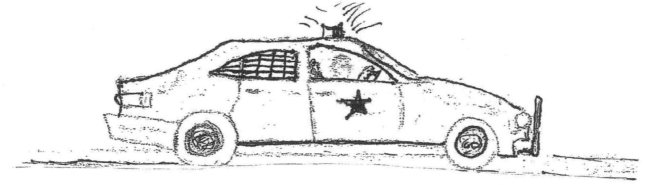

A man and a lady police officer slowly approached us. The man was pointing something at me until the lady said, "Put that away. Can't you see how friendly she is?"

The lady officer picked up the baby and gave it a hug and a kiss, then handed it to an ambulance lady.

The other offices checked my neck. And said, "No tag. You want me to call the pound, Sarge?"

The lady officer picked me up and gave me a kiss on the nose.

I wagged my tail and gave her a kiss back.

"No." She said, "she's coming home with me. We can't have a heroine locked up in the dog pound."

That's how I was introduced to Sergeant Sandy Simms.

Just before we got to the patrol car a man came over and patted Sandy on the back. "Good job, Sandy."

"I didn't do anything, Chief. It was this beautiful girl that deserves all the credit."

"The baby's parents agree with you on that. They want to give the dog's owner a 10,000 dollar reward for finding their stolen baby."

After about a 20 minute car ride, we stopped in front of a big house. On the way to the house Sandy sniffed me. "PU, you need a bath."

The bath was great! Sandy got her clothes all wet; finally, she gave up and jumped in.

Sandy and I were playing fetch in the back yard late that afternoon when the doorbell rang and never seemed to stop.

When the people heard that the parents of the baby wanted to give the owner of the poor lost dog a reward of 10,000 dollars, everyone came to claim me.

They patted their leg, snapped their fingers, whistled and called me all kinds of names. One of them even called me boy.

Then I heard Bill's voice. "I've come to get my dog Milly."

I didn't know what to do.

When Bill leaned forward to pet me, I dropped my tail and pressed myself against Sandy's leg.

"I'm sorry sir." Sandy said. "Can't you see you're scaring her. You have to go."

Halfway down the walkway Bill turned and shouted. "I'll see you in court, Lady!"

"Here comes Sandy, you better hide."

 "I want to know how this ends."

"When I come back, I'll tell you."

Fin jumped on Angel's nose. "You may not come back this way. I'm coming with you."

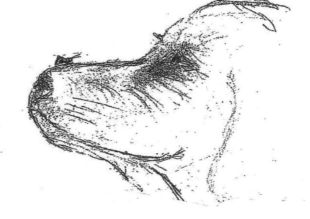

"Tilt your head and I'll slip under your ear."

As Sandy led Angel to the courtroom, Fin and Angel continued.

"How are you going to get back to your room?"

"I'll hop off at the water fountain."

"How do you know we'll stop there?"

"After they see the Judge, everybody is thirsty.

Oh, one more thing. If I tickle you, please don't scratch!"

Suddenly, the door flew open to a room filled with reporters and there looming above them sat Judge Abraham McGill. Angel had to strain her neck to see him.

The old Judge looked down, "Well Mister Hall, you asked for your day in court and here we are. Let's hear it."

Bill pointed, I went over to her house and she wouldn't give me my dog Milly."

"You mean Officer Simms?"

"Yes sir."

"Is that true Officer Simms?"

"Yes sir. The only thing he showed me was a picture of a puppy and when he approached to pet her, she became very nervous."

Bill held up the picture. "My wife will testify that Milly is our dog."

"Oh, I'm sure she will. Bailiff bring me the picture."

After studying the picture for several seconds, the judge held it up. "This is it?"

"Yes sir."

"No Bill of Sale?"

"No Sir."

"Mister Hall, the dog is over six months old. Where are her shot records and license? And just how did you plan on taking the dog home? Where is her collar and leash?"

Bill's mind flashed back to the woods where he had thrown them. "I ah...," he stuttered.

Pointing with his finger, Judge McGill commanded, "Officer Simms, bring the dog up here in front of me."

"Now Mister Hall come up here and claim your dog."

Fin peeked out from under Angel's ear.

As Bill came closer and closer Angel began to shake.

"" "Do something!"

Fin shouted.

Angel let out a growl that could be heard clear in the back of the courtroom. The Judge slammed down his gavel. "The dog will remain in the custody of Officer Simms until proven otherwise."

"But Judge!" Bill protested.

"Mister Hall, you may claim the dog is yours, but the dog just told this entire courtroom she's not."

As the courtroom cleared Sandy knelt down beside Angel. "Can I say something, sir?"

Judge McGill nodded. "Yes."

"Being a Police Officer, I'm not allowed to accept any rewards. If the parents still want to give the money to someone, I suggest the Humane Society for Lost and Abused Animals."

"What do you call her?"

"After what she did, Angel"

17

"That seems appropriate. You know what they say: Angels come in all shapes and sizes."

Sandy kissed Angel on the head. "They sure do!"

The Judge looked up from sorting some papers just as Sandy and Angel reached the door. He jerked his head back and blinked his eyes.

Was that?

Could it be?

It looked like there was a halo just above Angel's head. The Judge looked around the courtroom for someone to confirm his sighting, but there was no one.

When Sandy stopped at the water fountain in the hallway Fin boasted, "See, I told you!" Then he slipped from under Angel's ear and hopped to the floor.

Sandy looked down just as Angel nuzzled Fin. "I see you have found a new friend."

Angel looked up and barked.

Sandy bent down to have a closer look. "You know people say crickets are good luck" Angel barked and wagged her tail.

"Are you ready to go home?" Angel jumped up and licked Sandy's face.

"Come on then, let's go.""

Fin watched the pair until the outside door closed, then hopped behind the water fountain and made his way back to the holding cell.

19

Made in the USA
Middletown, DE
09 March 2023

26373957R00015